Karen's Ducklings

Also in the Babysitters Little Sister series:

Look out for:

Karen's Ducklings

Ann M. Martin

Illustrations by Susan Tang

Scholastic Children's Books,
Commonwealth House, 1-19 New Oxford Street,
London WC1A 1NU, UK
a division of Scholastic Ltd
London ~ New York ~ Toronto ~ Sydney ~ Auckland

First published in the US by Scholastic Inc., 1992
First published in the UK by Scholastic Ltd, 1996

ISBN 0 590 13342 X

Typeset by A.J. Latham Ltd, Dunstable, Beds.
Printed by Cox & Wyman Ltd, Reading, Berks.

10 9 8 7 6 5 4 3 2 1

*To everyone at Bedford Middle School,
especially Pat Brown,
. . . and to the real mother duck
who raised her babies in the courtyard.*

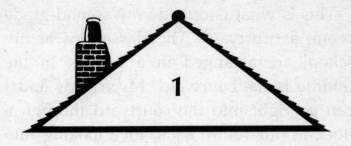

Springtime

I was looking out of the windows in my classroom. I was not daydreaming, though. I was *supposed* to be looking out of the windows. My teacher, Miss Colman, had told us to watch for signs of spring.

There were not too many signs yet. The branches of the trees and bushes showed some fat buds, but no little green leaves. The tips of flowers were just beginning to poke through the dirt in the gardens. And I had seen several robins. But . . . I wanted spring *now*.

I am not a very patient waiter.

This is what is outside my second-grade room: a courtyard. The classrooms at my school are arranged in a square. In the middle is the courtyard. My friends and I can go right into the courtyard through a door in our room. I just love looking into the yard. Flower gardens are everywhere. In the middle are some trees. There are lots of bushes, too, especially under the windows of the classrooms. Sometimes I see things moving in the bushes, usually birds and squirrels. Once I saw a chipmunk.

My classmates and I were very busy getting ready for spring. We were studying the season.

"What does spring make you think of?" Miss Colman had asked us.

"Plants," said Hannie Papadakis. She is one of my two best friends.

"Warm weather," said Nancy Dawes. She is my other best friend.

"Baby animals!" I shouted.

"Indoor voice, Karen," Miss Colman reminded me.

In my classroom were all sorts of spring projects. Miss Colman had given each of us an empty milk carton, some dirt and some seeds. We had planted zinnias. We were waiting for our flowers to grow. We were going to make a spring bulletin board. It would be very beautiful. (I said we should use cotton wool to make puffy clouds.) We were learning about animal families and animal babies. Miss Colman had said we would make something called a terrarium, but I did not know what that was.

Also we were writing stories and poems about spring. This was my best poem (I wrote it without any help):

SPRING, SPRING.
A VERY GOOD THING.
IT MAKES ME WANT TO
SING AND SING.

BY KAREN BREWER, AGE 7

Miss Colman put my poem on the wall. I was proud of that. In a few weeks, my class was going to celebrate Spring Day. The kids in the other second-grade class were going to come into our room. We were going to show them our spring things and tell them about them too. Our bulletin board would be ready. Our zinnias would be in bloom (we hoped), and our terrarium (whatever that was) would be finished.

Spring would not be just in our classroom, though. It would be everywhere in Stoneybrook, Connecticut. (That is where I live.) It would be in the courtyard outside our windows. It would be in parks and fields and woods. And it would be at my mother's house and at my father's house. Mummy has a little garden with lots of trees and a couple of flowerbeds. Daddy has a gigundo garden with a few trees and tons of flowerbeds. I like to watch spring come to both of my gardens.

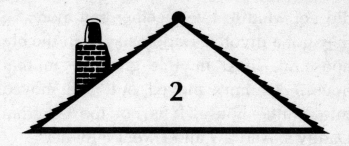

Spring Has Sprung

Why do I have two gardens and two houses? Because I have two families.

My name is Karen Brewer. I have just turned seven. I love a lot of things, like the people in my families, and holidays, and animals. Also, I love school, and Miss Colman, and spring. I could not wait to watch for signs of spring in both of my gardens.

Here is how I got two families. A long time ago, I had just one family – Mummy; Daddy; my little brother, Andrew; and me.

Then Mummy and Daddy decided that they did not want to live together any more. So they got a divorce. Daddy stayed in the big house we lived in. (He grew up in that house.) Mummy moved out. She moved into a little house. It is not too far from Daddy's. Andrew and I went with her.

After a while Mummy and Daddy each got married again, but not to each other. Mummy married Seth Engle. He is my stepfather. He moved into the little house, and he brought along his dog, Midgie, and his cat, Rocky. Mostly, Andrew and I live with Mummy and Seth at the little house. (I have a pet rat there. Her name is Emily Junior.)

But every other weekend and on certain holidays we live at the big house with Daddy and our stepmother. Our stepmother is Elizabeth. Guess what. Elizabeth has *four* children. They are our stepbrothers and stepsister – Charlie, Sam, David Michael and Kristy. They are all older than Andrew and me. Even David Michael, who is seven. (He is almost eight, and I am not.)

So many people live at the big house! There is also Nannie, who is Elizabeth's mother, so she is my stepgrandmother. And there is Emily Michelle, who is my adopted sister. Daddy and Elizabeth adopted her from a faraway country called Vietnam. A bunch of pets live at the big house, too – a cat, a dog, and two goldfish.

I have special nicknames for my brother and me. I call us Andrew Two-Two and Karen Two-Two. (Once, Miss Colman read a book to our class. It was called *Jacob Two-Two Meets the Hooded Fang*. That's where I got our nicknames.) We are two-twos because we have two of so many things. We have two houses and two families, two mummies and two daddies, two cats and two dogs. We each have two bedrooms, one at Mummy's little house and one at Daddy's big house. I have two bicycles, one at each house. I have two stuffed cats that look just the same. Moosie stays at the big house, Goosie stays at the little house. I even have my two best friends. Hannie lives across the street from Daddy and one house down. Nancy lives next door to Mummy.

This is what would happen when spring came to my two houses. At Mummy's, the pink flowers on the dogwood tree would bloom. The yellow flowers on the forsythia bushes would bloom. The big pink-and-white flowers on the magnolia tree would bloom. The bunched-up purple flowers on the lilac bush would bloom. (Lilac flowers smell gigundoly wonderful. I would pick a bouquet for Miss Colman.)

At Daddy's, forsythia bushes would bloom, too. In his garden, the flowers would poke up through the dirt. First would come little white snowdrops and yellow or purple crocus buds. Later would come yellow daffodils and yellow-and-white narcissus, and tulips and hyacinths in all sorts of colours. And even later, the azaleas would bloom, and so would the fat peony flowers. Maybe I would take some pictures of my two gardens for Spring Day. Then I could show Miss Colman lots of signs of spring.

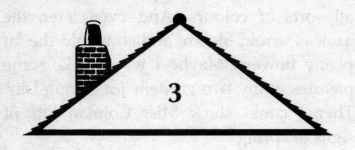

3

The Cool Car

I really like the word *grout*. It sounds just like *growl*, except with a "t" at the end, instead of an "l". You know what grout is? It is the white goo you use when you are making a picture out of tiles. It is the stuff you spread in between the tiles to hold them together.

Mummy and Seth had given me some grout and a whole bunch of tiles. So one day after school I was busy making a spring mosaic. (A mosaic is a tile design.) I was working at the table in the playroom of the

little house. Andrew was in the playroom, too. He was building a fire station out of his red Lego. While he built, he made fire-truck noises. He sang, *"Ooooo-eeeee-ooooo, ning-ning-ning-ning. Oooo-eeee-ooooo."*

In the background, *Sesame Street* was on the TV. Andrew just adores *Sesame Street*. But he was not paying attention to it. Neither was I. We were too busy with our projects.

"Ning-ning-ning," Andrew sang.

"Hum, de-hum," I sang.

My mosaic was growing bigger.

So was Andrew's fire station. He was almost out of red Lego.

Sesame Street ended. Andrew turned the channel on the TV. He turned it again and again. *Flip, flip, flip.*

"Hey, Karen," he said a moment later.

"Yeah?" I did not glance up from my mosaic. I was working busily.

"Karen, look! Look at the TV! Look at that car!" cried Andrew.

12

I looked. On the TV screen was an advert for a toy car. It was a remote-control car. The ad showed a boy and girl making the car zip all around their house. When the car ran into something, it flipped over. Then it zoomed off again. The headlights really turned on.

"That is so cool!" exclaimed my brother.

"It's okay," I said. I went back to my mosaic.

"Hey, Karen, we can order the car through the post! And – and we do not have to pay for it until it comes. Oh, please, let's order it!"

"Andrew, I –"

"They are going to put the address on the TV!" shrieked Andrew. "Karen, write it down! Write it down!" Andrew shoved a piece of paper and a green crayon at me.

I had to write very, very fast. While I wrote, Andrew jumped up and down next to my table. "Did you get it?" he cried.

13

"I think so," I answered. I *hoped* so, because the advert was over.

"Goody. We have to send away for that car right now."

"I don't know, Andrew. How much did it cost?"

"Two dollars."

"Are you sure?" I asked. "That does not sound like very much money."

My brother looked offended. "I know a two when I see one," he replied.

"Sorry." I stopped to think. Then I said, "I am not sure if kids can order stuff through the post. I do not know if they are allowed."

"Oh, *please*? Please, please, puh-LEASE? Um, I think Seth might want the car. I really do. We could give it to him for Father's Day."

"We-ell . . ."

"Pretty please with a cherry on top?" begged Andrew.

"Okay," I said finally. Andrew and I had two dollars. That was no problem. But I

14

still did not know if a seven-year-old could order the car. So I wrote a letter to the address on the TV. I ordered one car. Then I signed Mummy's name to the letter. I thought that was safe, since Mummy is a grown-up.

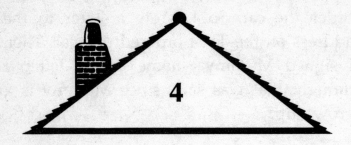

Mama Duck

Early one Monday morning I stood at the windows in Miss Colman's room. I was looking into the courtyard. I had found more signs of spring. I saw the tips of some yellow crocus flowers. I saw the tips of some purple crocus flowers and also some white crocus flowers. The green daffodil shoots were growing longer. So were the tulip shoots.

Something moved the bushes in one of the gardens. I pressed my face to a window. Maybe I would see another chipmunk.

No. No little striped body ran out. The bushes kept moving.

I kept watching.

A breeze blew aside the branches of the shrubs. And I saw . . . a duck.

"Hey!" I screamed. "There's a duck in the garden!"

"Oh, Karen," said Hannie.

"No, there really is! I just saw it. It's in those bushes."

Hannie and about six other kids raced to the windows. They crowded around me. I pointed to the bush I had seen moving. "He's right in there," I whispered. But nothing moved. No duck waddled into the courtyard. Everything was still and quiet.

"Karen," said Bobby Gianelli, who is *not* my best friend, "there is no duck. There is nothing. You are just crazy."

"I am not crazy! And there is too a duck!"

"Boys and girls?" said Miss Colman's voice. "What is going on?"

"Oh, Miss Colman!" I cried. I ran to her desk. Miss Colman put her things down.

17

She took off her coat. "There is a duck in the courtyard!" I exclaimed. "Honest. I just saw him. Only no one believes me."

"A duck," repeated Miss Colman. "What would a duck be doing here?" She peered out the window. "I can't see anything."

"But it is *there*!" I cried.

"Okay," said my teacher gently. "Show me."

Miss Colman opened the door to the courtyard. She went outside. I followed her. I walked right to the place where I had seen the duck. I pulled the branches of the bush aside. And there was a mummy duck sitting on a big nest of eggs.

"Oh, my goodness," said Miss Colman.

I stood and stared. I knew I had seen a duck, but I did not know I had seen a mother duck and her eggs.

From behind me came a lot of noise. The kids in my class were running outside. They wanted to get a better look at the duck. But Miss Colman said, "Inside, everybody!

Right now. Don't go near the duck. We do not want to frighten her."

Boy, was the rest of the day exciting. Miss Colman told the principal about the duck. She talked to a lot of the teachers. One teacher said, "You should call SAPA. That is the Small Animal Protection Agency. The people at SAPA will be able to tell you about wild ducks."

So Miss Colman telephoned SAPA. She told the man who answered the phone about Mama Duck. (That's what my friends and I were calling her.) Then Miss Colman said to our class, "Mama Duck must have got lost. She landed in our garden and began to lay her eggs. She has probably been here for a while already. We must let Mama Duck hatch her eggs and raise her ducklings by herself. We cannot touch her or her babies. But we can watch the ducklings hatch and grow!"

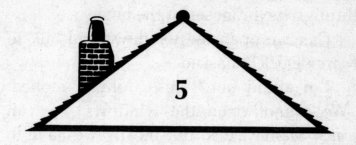

A Name for Mama Duck

When I went into my classroom the next morning, a big sign was on the door to the courtyard. It said, DO NOT ENTER!

"That is to remind us," Miss Colman told me, "not to go into the courtyard. We have to give Mama Duck her privacy. The only people who may go into the yard are a few teachers. They will bring Mama Duck water or anything she might need. They will be following special instructions from the people at SAPA."

Well, that was a bit disappointing. I

had thought we could watch Mama Duck through the branches of the bush.

"Can we open the windows and talk to Mama Duck?" I asked.

"I'm afraid not," Miss Colman replied. "We cannot open the windows. We can *watch* Mama Duck, but mostly we have to leave her alone."

Boo.

That morning we got to go to the school hall. We were having an assembly. The whole school was there. I just love assemblies.

This is how we sit at assemblies. In the very front are the nursery classes. Behind them are the kids in first grade. Behind the first-graders sit my friends and I. And so on. The big fifth-graders sit at the very back of the room.

That morning I sat between Hannie and Nancy. We did not know why we were having an assembly, but Miss Colman said it was for a special reason. She said we would feel very proud.

When the assembly began, guess who walked on to the stage. Miss Colman!

"Good morning," she said. "As many of you know, our school has an unusual guest. Our guest will be staying here for a while." Miss Colman told everyone about Mama Duck. She even said that I was the one who had first seen her. Then she talked about calling the people at SAPA. She said we could watch Mama Duck from our classrooms, but that we could not go into the courtyard. She said it was very important to let Mama Duck raise her babies by herself. Mama Duck would know best.

When Miss Colman finished talking, the head walked on to the stage. She said, "I have been thinking that it might be fun to give our mama duck a real name. Of course, since Karen Brewer found the duck, our guest officially belongs to Miss Colman's class. But we will all be watching her and her babies, so everyone should have a chance to name her. We are going to have a duck-naming contest. Right now. Your teachers are handing out slips of paper. I would like each of you to write down one name for our duck. No jokes, please. This afternoon I will put all the names in a box and choose one. That will be our duck's new name."

"Cool," I said to Nancy. "I think our duck should be named Jemima. Like Jemima Puddleduck in the book."

"I think she should just be called Mama Duck," said Nancy.

Ricky Torres was sitting behind me. "*I* think she should be named Stinky," he said. He began to laugh.

I turned around. "Ricky," I exclaimed. "That is not nice. Mama Duck isn't stinky. And anyway, joke names are not allowed. Remember?"

Ricky stuck his tongue out at me, and I stuck mine out at him. Then I carefully wrote JEMIMA on my paper. Nancy wrote MAMA DUCK. Hannie wrote QUACKER. I did not know what Ricky wrote, and I did not care.

24

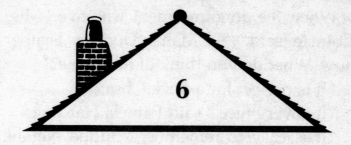

Feather

"Attention, please. May I have your attention, please?"

Our head's voice came over the intercom.

My friends and I stopped talking. Miss Colman stopped writing on the blackboard. Ricky took the spitball out of his mouth.

It was Tuesday afternoon. Our assembly had been held that morning.

"Boys and girls, our mother duck has a new name. I have just chosen a piece of paper. The winning name is Feather."

"Oh, cute," I whispered.

When the announcement was over, Miss Colman said, "So Mama Duck is Feather now. What do you think of her name?"

"It is perfect for a duck," I said.

"It is very nice," said Pamela Harding.

"It is easy to remember," added Natalie Springer.

I gazed through a window. I had not seen Feather all day. And I could not see her then. Miss Colman had told me not to worry, though. "Your duck is hiding," she had said. "She is busy taking care of her eggs. She has to keep them warm."

I understood that. But I wished Feather did not need quite so much privacy. I wanted to be her friend.

I turned away from the window. I realized Miss Colman was talking to us, and I had not been paying attention.

". . . another project for Spring Day," she was saying.

I nudged Ricky. "What?" I whispered.

"Spring Day," he hissed.

He was no help.

"Since we have discovered Feather," Miss Colman went on, "I thought it might be fun to write about her and her babies. We can watch Feather every day. And we can take turns keeping a diary for her. We can write about what happens when she hatches her eggs, and when the ducklings start to grow up. We can take photos of Feather, too." Miss Colman glanced at me and then added quickly, "Through the windows, of course. And you can draw pictures of Feather. We can use the photos and pictures to illustrate our story. We will make a real book. When it is finished, we will take it to the library, and guess what. Mr Counts will put it with the rest of the books, so other kids can borrow it."

Mr Counts is our librarian.

I thought this idea was so, so cool. My classmates and I would be authors! We would write a book, and it would go in our library, and everybody could borrow it and read it.

We would be famous at Stoneybrook Academy.

Nancy raised her hand. "May we start the book today?" she asked.

"I think that is a very good idea," Miss Colman answered. "Who would like to write the first entry in Feather's diary?"

Every single kid in my class raised his or her hand.

"My goodness," said Miss Colman. She closed her eyes. Then she pointed to a name in her register. She opened her eyes. "Natalie Springer," she said. "Natalie, you may write about Feather today."

Miss Colman gave Natalie a big piece of paper. Natalie wrote, "Today is Tuesday. Yistirday Karen Brear founded a mummy duck in the garden. Today the ducks name is Fither." (Miss Colman made Natalie correct that.) "Feather is sitting on a nest she is going to hatch her eggs."

That was the beginning of *Feather's Story*.

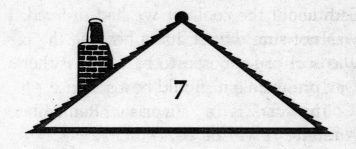

7

Bad News

"Mummy, is the post here?" I shouted. I ran into the little house after school on Monday afternoon.

"Indoor voice, Karen," Mummy reminded me.

I wish grown-ups did not say that to me so often.

Andrew ran out of the playroom. He met me in the hall. "Karen, the post is late!" he announced. "Let's go and wait for it together. Maybe the car has come."

"*SHH!*" I hissed.

Andrew and I had not told Mummy or Seth about the cool car we had ordered. I was not sure why. I guess because the car was sort of supposed to be Seth's Father's Day present. So it should be a surprise.

"The car is a surprise. Remember, Andrew?" I whispered.

"Oh, yeah," he whispered back.

Andrew and I went outside. We sat on the front steps. I shaded my eyes and peered down the street.

"No post truck," I said.

"Boo," said Andrew. "I want to play with that cool car."

"I thought the car was for Seth," I said.

"Oh. It is. But of course we will have to test it first," said my brother.

"Of course."

It was Andrew's turn to look down the street. "There is the truck!" he yelled.

Andrew and I jumped up. We ran to the mailbox. We waited for the truck to arrive. Soon it stopped in front of us. Its brakes squeaked.

"Here is your post," said our letter carrier. She handed Andrew a stack of envelopes. "Oh, and one other thing," she added.

She handed me a box. Then she drove off.

The box was for Lisa Engle. (That is Mummy.) It was from the Custom Car Company. "It's the car!" I cried. "It came!"

Andrew and I sat down in the middle of our garden. We tore open the box. Inside was a beautiful car, just like the one we had seen on TV.

"And it is red!" exclaimed Andrew. "Okay. Let's make it work."

"Wait. I think it needs batteries," I said.

"I will get them!" Andrew grabbed the rest of the post. He ran to the house with it. "I will not tell Mummy Seth's present is here!" he called to me.

While Andrew was inside, I looked through the box. I found a letter. This must tell us how to pay the two dollars, I thought. I opened the envelope. I pulled

31

out the letter. At the top, it said, INVOICE. (I was not sure what that meant.) Underneath, it said, "Please pay the following: $20.00 – one Custom Car, plus $3.95 – shipping and handling."

YIKES! Andrew and I did not owe the car company two dollars. We owed them twenty dollars! Andrew must have read the ad wrong. Plus, we owed them the shipping and handling money.

What were we going to do?

I was still staring at the letter when Andrew ran back outside.

"I've got the batteries!" he said.

In a flash, Andrew had put the batteries in the $23.95 car. He found the remote control. He put the car on the driveway.

"Don't you think we should read the directions?" I asked.

"Nah," Andrew answered. He pressed a button. The car shot up the driveway. It crashed into a fence post.

It fell apart.

"Oh, no!" I cried.

Andrew and I fussed over the car for a very long time. We even read the directions. But we could not make the car work again. So we hid it in my wardrobe. We hid the letter, too. "Do not tell Mummy or Seth about this," I said to Andrew.

"I won't," he promised.

I felt *awful*.

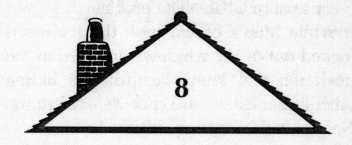

Sitting Around

"Karen, today it is your turn to write about Feather for our book," said Miss Colman. "Remember to watch for her."

"Okay," I replied.

A week had gone by since Andrew and I had wrecked the cool car. Really, Andrew had wrecked it, but that was partly my fault. I should have read the instructions to him. But I had been too upset about the letter.

I was still upset. The Custom Car Company was waiting for their $23.95. But

Andrew and I did not have that much money.

This was a GIGUNDO problem.

While Miss Colman took the register, I looked out of the windows. I looked at the bush where I knew Feather was hiding with her nest. I did not see anything. *Nobody* had seen very much. Feather was just sitting on the nest, keeping her eggs warm. If she got up to exercise or something, my friends and I did not see. Maybe Feather roamed around at night, when she was alone.

Anyway, *Feather's Story* was very boring so far.

We tried to be nice about this. Yesterday, Jannie Gilbert had written about Feather. She had said, "Feather is buzy taking car of her eggs."

The day before that, Hank Reubens had written, "Feather is still sitting on her eggs. Keeping them worm. I think she is a good duck mother."

I felt bad about the cool car and the $23.95. But do you know what made me feel a little better? Spring. My two gardens looked springier every day. And my classroom looked *very* springy.

We had started working on our bulletin board. Across the top were letters that spelled SPRING IS HERE! Jannie and Pamela had cut out the letters. (At first they had lost the R's. For a while the letters spelled SPING IS HEE!) Under the letters were spring poems we had written. We had been working on poetry almost every day. I especially liked writing haikus. This was my spring haiku:

THE BROWN EARTH IS WARM
FROM THE SPRING SUNSHINE. FLOWERS
GROW AND BLOOM, THEN WILT.

Miss Colman had chosen that haiku for the board.

Across the bottom of the bulletin board were paper flowers we had made in art class. Each of us had made a different kind

37

of flower. A zinnia, a marigold, a violet, a petunia, a lady's slipper. I had made a daisy. (Actually I had made two. But I had ruined the first one. I had played "He loves me, he loves me not..." and torn off the petals.)

A new spring thing was sitting on one of the windowsills. It was our terrarium. This is how a terrarium works. You take a glass bowl or a small aquarium and you put in some dirt and then you put in some nice damp moss and some other shade plants like little ferns and maybe some violets. You water the plants, then you cover your terrarium with a piece of glass and . . . it takes care of itself! The water collects on the glass top and "rains" back down on the plants. All you have to do is look at your terrarium and watch the plants grow.

Oh! Our other plants were growing, too. Our flower seeds were sprouting in their milk-carton gardens. They had not bloomed yet, but they looked green and pretty. Miss Colman said the buds would come soon.

I thought about Feather. I had not seen her that day. So I wrote, "Today Feather is just sitting around. Her eggs must be extra warm now."

Miss Colman said, "I think Feather's eggs will hatch soon."

I hoped she was right. I was tired of waiting.

9

The Mysterious Bill

"Glug, glug, glug," said Andrew. He was pretending to chug his milk. When he put down his glass, I saw a milk moustache. "I am an old man," said Andrew. "I have white whiskers. Oh, I am so old."

"Andrew, wipe your mouth. You are in the dining room," I reminded him.

At the little house (and also at the big house) we usually eat in the kitchen. But sometimes we eat in the dining room. In the dining room, we are supposed to be on our best behaviour. Milk moustaches are not part of good behaviour.

It was dinnertime at the little house. Mummy and Andrew and Seth and I were eating salad and lasagne. Seth had got home late.

"Anything interesting in the post?" asked Seth.

"Nope," Andrew said.

"The *TV Guide*," I said.

"A very strange letter," Mummy said.

"Ooh, a mystery!" I exclaimed. "What did the strange letter say, Mummy?"

"A letter for you?" Seth asked Mummy.

"Yes," she answered. "It was addressed to Lisa Engle. And it was from the Custom Car Company in Indiana."

"The Custom Car Company?" Seth repeated.

Uh-oh. I glanced at Andrew. Since he is only four, he did not understand that anything was wrong. Not yet, anyway.

Mummy nodded. "A car company. The

letter was from a Mr Simpson. He says I owe him twenty-three dollars and ninety-five cents. For a car. Who ever heard of a car that costs only twenty-three ninety-five?"

(Across the table, Andrew choked on his milk.)

"Maybe Mr Simpson meant twenty-three *hundred* and ninety-five?" said Seth.

"Maybe," replied Mummy doubtfully.

"No," said Andrew. "He – "

I interrupted Andrew. I gave him a Look. "It must have been a mistake," I said loudly. "Maybe you owe twenty-three ninety-five for a, um, jar."

"I have not ordered any jars," said Mummy. "I suppose Mr Simpson could have sent the bill to the wrong Lisa Engle."

"That must be it," agreed Seth. "Don't worry about the letter."

"I won't," said Mummy. "I have already thrown it away."

Whew. Well, that was good.

Still, I felt . . . funny. I had got Mummy in trouble.

When dinner was over, I pulled Andrew into my room. "We have to talk about the car," I said to him.

"The fool car?" (Andrew said "fool car" now instead of "cool car".)

"Yes, the fool car. I did not know the Custom Car Company would send *another* letter. And of course it was addressed to Mummy, so she opened it. I wonder if more letters will come."

"Maybe we should try to get the post every day," suggested Andrew.

"We can't. Sometimes it comes while we are at school. Or while we are at the big house."

"We could write a letter to Mr Simpson."

"But what would we tell him?" I asked. "We've broken his car."

"Yeah," said Andrew. He stared at the floor.

"This is a tragedy," I said sadly.

"Yeah," Andrew said again, even though

I am sure he did not know what that meant. "A tradegy."

"I think we have done something really wrong," I added.

Andrew's eyes grew huge. "Will we have to go to jail?"

"I am pretty sure the police do not put children in jail," I said.

I wished I were one hundred per cent sure.

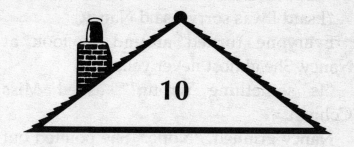

Seven Duck Babies

One morning we were working in our maths workbooks. I was subtracting nines. That is hard for me. It is hard for Ricky, too. I looked over at him. He was working with his tongue poking out of his mouth.

Our classroom was very quiet. Everyone was busy.

Suddenly someone yelled, "Hey, look!"

I jumped a mile. My pencil rolled off my desk.

"Nancy!" exclaimed Miss Colman.

"Oh, I'm sorry," said Nancy, "but – "

45

"You scared me," I announced.

"I said I was sorry," said Nancy.

Everyone turned around to look at Nancy. She almost never yells.

"Is something wrong?" asked Miss Colman.

Nancy grinned. "Nope." She pointed out of one of the windows. "I think something is happening at Feather's nest. The bushes keep moving."

"The babies!" Natalie cried.

"The ducklings!" I cried.

Even Miss Colman got excited. "The eggs!" she cried. She dashed to the windows and looked outside. "I think Feather is hatching her eggs."

We are not supposed to leave our desks. Not in the middle of maths-workbook time. And especially not without asking first. Even so, every kid in my class – including me – flew to the windows. We leaned over the sills and stared outside. We were very crowded. This girl named Audrey tried to shove in front of me.

"Hey!" I exclaimed.

"Move over!" said Audrey. "I want to see."

"Well, so do I."

But there was not much to see. Feather stayed in the bushes.

"All right, class," said Miss Colman. "Let's take our seats."

We sat down again. But all during the day, we kept looking out of the windows. Even Miss Colman did. Once, I was able to see in the bushes.

"There are the babies!" I shrieked. "I saw some babies."

After lunch, one of the teachers and a man from SAPA went into the courtyard. They looked at Feather's nest. They were careful not to touch anything and to be very quiet. When they came back inside, the man said, "Your duck has hatched seven eggs. The ducklings seem to be fine. You will probably see them sometime tomorrow. Today they are resting and drying off. Tomorrow they will start to walk around."

"Gosh," I said to Hannie. "Duck babies sure learn how to walk fast. People babies cannot walk when they are just one day old."

"I know," said Hannie. "Oh, boy. Tomorrow is going to be exciting. We will see the ducklings for real."

"I wonder how fast ducklings grow up," I said. "And I wonder who will take the babies. Maybe they will go to a farm together. Or maybe they will go to seven different homes, even though that would be sad."

"Karen – " Hannie started to say. She was frowning.

But Miss Colman began to talk then too. "Someone has a very important job today," she said. "Who is supposed to add to *Feather's Story?*"

"Oh, I am!" exclaimed Bobby. And he wrote, "Today Feather hathed her babies!!! She had seven ducklings!! The man said they look helthy. We have not seen them much but we might see them tomoroe.

They can alredy walk. I think they are smart. I do not know if they are cute."

We will know tomorrow, I thought. I could not wait to see the ducklings waddling around the courtyard. I wondered if they would come near the windows so we could see them up close. I hoped they were not going to be as shy as their mother was.

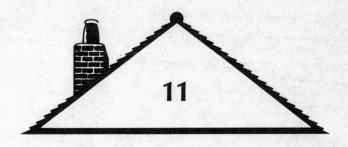

Making Way for Ducklings

"Look! They are so cute!"

"They're fuzzy!"

"They are so little!"

It was the next day. I had reached school early. Even Miss Colman had not arrived yet. I was standing at the windows with Nancy, Leslie, Tammy and Terri (they are twins), Ricky, Jannie and Hank.

Guess what we were looking at.

The ducklings!

Feather had brought them out from under the bushes. She was leading them all

through the courtyard. They followed her in a line.

"She is showing them around," said Ricky.

"No, I think she is showing them *off*," I said.

The ducklings really were pretty cute. They were small and fuzzy. They followed Feather wherever she went. They walked and waddled and hopped. I could not believe that just a day earlier they had still been inside their eggs. They looked as if they had been waddling around the garden for years.

"You know what?" said Tammy. "We gave Feather a name, so we should give the ducklings names, too."

"Should we have another contest?" asked Hank.

"Maybe," said Tammy. "Or we could just name them ourselves."

"But they look exactly alike," said Terri. "We cannot tell them apart."

"So?" said Jannie.

"Yeah, that doesn't matter," I agreed. "Let's think of seven duckling names."

"How about Happy, Dopey, Grumpy, Sleepy, Sneezy, Doc and Bashful?" suggested Leslie. She looked pleased with herself.

"But they were seven dwarfs," I pointed out. "We have seven ducks."

"Well," began Ricky, "we could call them Daffy, Donald, Huey, Dewey . . . and . . . hmm, I cannot think of three more duck names."

"I can!" I cried. "How about the names of Mrs Mallard's babies in *Make Way for Ducklings?* I think she had eight babies. We could use seven of those names."

We found a copy of *Make Way for Ducklings.* I turned to the part where Mrs Mallard names her babies. "Here it is," I said. "She named them Jack, Kack, Lack, Mack, Nack, Oack, Pack, and Quack. We could use the first seven names. What do you think?"

Everyone liked the idea. When Miss

Colman arrived, she liked it, too.

For a while that morning, Miss Colman and my classmates and I stood at the windows and watched Feather and her babies. We could see other kids in other windows watching, too. Feather had a big audience.

That day it was Hannie's turn to write in *Feather's Story*. Of course, she wrote about the ducklings and what they were doing. "The babies waddle around just like there mother. They followe her. The ducklings are fuzzy. They do not have feathers like Feather yet."

At break I did not play outside. I stayed in our classroom with Miss Colman. I drew a picture of Feather, Jack, Kack, Lack, Mack, Nack, Oack, and Pack. I coloured it carefully. It was for our book.

"Perfect," said Miss Colman. "I will try to take some photos today. We can put them in the book, too."

"Oh, yes!" I exclaimed. "And then everybody will know what the babies looked like when they were not even two days old."

That afternoon, Miss Colman did take some pictures, even though Feather mostly hid her babies.

"She is protecting them," Miss Colman told us. "She is being a good mother."

So Hannie added that to *Feather's Story*.

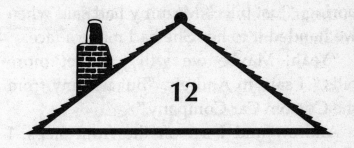

12

The Next Letter

When I came home from school that afternoon, Andrew was waiting for me. "Karen!" he whispered loudly. "The post has not come yet. Let's try to get it before Mummy does." Andrew glanced over his shoulder.

I looked too. I could not see Mummy. Even so, I whispered back to him, "Be careful. I am still worried about the police."

"Probably we will not get a letter," Andrew replied.

That was true. We had waited for the

post the day before. The post had been very boring. "Just bills," Mummy had said when we handed it to her. She had made a face.

"Yeah. Maybe we will just get more bills," I said to Andrew. "But not any from the Custom Car Company."

Andrew and I sat on the front steps. I kept looking at my watch.

"The post is *really* late today," I said.

"Maybe it will not come at all," Andrew said.

Squeak, squeak. Just then we heard the squeaky brakes of the post truck.

"Uh-oh." I took Andrew by the hand. We walked slowly to our mailbox. The letter carrier handed us a stack of envelopes.

"Thank you," whispered Andrew.

"Thank you," I whispered.

"You're welcome," whispered the letter carrier. Then she drove off.

Andrew looked at me. "Read the envelopes, Karen," he said.

"Okay. A letter from Granny. A bill from the phone company. A bill from the electric

company. An ad. A letter from the Custom Car Company. . ." I glanced at my brother. "The Custom Car Company," I repeated.

"Read it."

"It is addressed to Mummy." Andrew did not say anything. "But I guess it is really for us," I went on. I opened the envelope. Inside was a letter. It said: "Dear Mrs Engle, Our records show that you owe $23.95 for one red Custom Car. Please pay this sum promptly. This is the last letter you will receive."

The letter went on, but I did not bother to read it. (I saw Mr Simpson's name at the bottom, though.)

"Andrew!" I exclaimed. "This is the last letter Mr Simpson is going to send! All we have to do is throw it away. We will never hear from the Custom Car Company again."

"Yes!" cried Andrew.

My brother and I ran inside. We gave the post to Mummy. Except for the Awful Letter. We took that upstairs. I *almost* threw it away.

But at the last moment I hid it. I put it with the broken Custom Car.

"Andrew," I said, "I feel funny about this. The Custom Car Company sent us a car. But we did not send them back anything. Not even one cent."

"Maybe we could get the money." Andrew looked thoughtful.

"Maybe," I agreed. "How much do you have?"

Andrew checked his piggy bank. "Two quarters," he replied.

I checked my piggy bank. "I have two dollars and eighty cents. Let me see. Together we have three dollars and thirty cents."

"Is that good?"

"Not really. We still need over twenty dollars."

"Let's look in the couch!" said Andrew.

I guess he was looking for a twenty-dollar bill. He found a dime.

"Okay, let's look in coat pockets," he suggested.

We felt around in every pocket of every coat in the house. We found more than one dollar, which was a surprise.

"Is *that* good?" asked my brother.

"Not good enough," I answered.

Andrew said he was getting a headache. I told him I already had a stomachache.

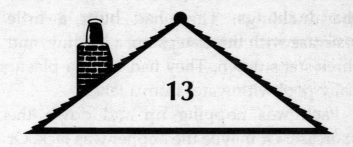

13

One Little Duckling

Hop, hop, hop, rest, hop, hop, hop.

"Pack is very talented," I said.

"How do you know that's Pack?" asked Nancy.

"I don't," I replied. "But maybe it is."

Nancy and I were standing at the windows of our classroom. We were watching Feather's ducklings. They were still downy, but they were growing bigger. And more adventurous. Now they explored the courtyard without their mother. My friends and I saw them everywhere.

The teachers had made a playground for the ducklings. They had built a little staircase with three steps up, a landing, and three steps down. They had filled a plastic baby pool with water from a lake.

Pack was hopping up and down the staircase. Or maybe the hopper was Jack. Or Kack. Or Lack or Mack or Nack or Oack. The ducklings still looked alike. Except for one. One duckling was smaller than the others. And slower. Sometimes he swam in the pool. But he could not hop up and down the staircase. Mostly, he hung around in the bushes with Feather. I always looked for the one little duckling. I just liked to keep my eye on him.

Hannie joined Nancy and me by the windows. "The ducklings are much more fun now," she said. "I mean, now that they are growing up. Feather does not protect them so much any more."

"Except when someone comes into the courtyard," I said. Every time a teacher went into the courtyard with a new toy or to add water to the pool, Feather would hurry her babies into the bushes. But when the teacher left, the ducklings would run out again. They liked to play.

"Where is the little duckling?" asked Nancy.

"With Feather, I think," I said. "When I got to school this morning, four ducklings were in the pool, and two were climbing the steps. I thought I saw another in the bushes. It must have been the little one."

It was my turn to add to *Feather's Story*, so that day I wrote: "The ducklings are getting bigger. They run everywhere well six of them do. The little duckling does not run around to much. I think he is the runt of the litter. Like Wilbur in *Charlottes Web*. Maybe one day he will be as famouse as Wilbur got to be. Maybe he will go on TV."

I drew another picture to illustrate the book. I drew a picture of a TV. On the TV screen was a duck. Underneath the duck I wrote, THE WORLD FAMOUSE DUCKLING.

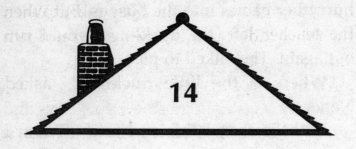

14

Saying Goodbye

I liked my entry in *Feather's Story*. It was a happy entry.

The next day's entry was very, very sad.

Audrey wrote it. She wrote: "Today we found out that one duckling died. We gave him a funeral. We feel bad. That is all I have to say."

Miss Colman came to our classroom early that morning. Usually a lot of kids get there before she does. But not that day. When Nancy and I skipped into the room, Miss Colman was sitting at her desk. She looked so sad that Nancy and I sat at our desks, too. We did not talk to each other. When the other kids came in, they also sat down and did not talk.

We knew something was wrong.

Finally Miss Colman stood up. "Boys and girls," she said, "I have some sad news. Last night the little duckling died. Mr Berger found him this morning." (Mr Berger is a teacher. His classroom is next door to my classroom.) "We think the duckling had been sick. That is probably why he was so little."

I began to cry. But I raised my hand anyway. "What about the other ducklings?" I asked. "What about Feather?"

"The other ducklings seem fine. Feather, too." Miss Colman smiled. "Look outside and see for yourselves."

My friends and I turned towards the windows. There was Feather. She was waddling through the courtyard. In a line behind her waddled six ducklings.

"Feather does not look very sad," I said.

"Doesn't she care about Jack?"

"Jack?" repeated Miss Colman.

"The little duckling," I said. "I think that one was Jack."

"Oh," replied Miss Colman. "Well, I am sure Feather is sad, but she also knows she has plenty of work to do. She has to take care of her other babies. Do you feel sad, Karen?"

I nodded. "The ducklings are sort of our pets."

"Yeah," said Hannie, sniffling.

All around me, kids had started to cry. I think even Miss Colman cried a little. She had to keep taking off her glasses and dabbing her eyes with a tissue. "You know," said my teacher, "it is okay to feel sad when someone or something dies."

I raised my hand. "Miss Colman? When Louie, our collie dog, died, we gave him a memorial service. And when my first goldfish died, we buried her in the backyard. We gave her a funeral."

"We all went to the funeral," added Natalie. "It was a nice thing to do for Crystal Light. And when it was over, we felt a little better."

"Would you like to have a memorial service for the duckling?" asked Miss Colman.

"Yes," said my friends and I.

That day, instead of writing in our workbooks, or reading, or subtracting nines, we planned a memorial service for Jack the duckling. First, we each drew a picture of Jack. Then we wrote something about him. I wrote: "I will always remember how Jack hid in the bushes with Feather. He was very sweet. I will miss Jack. So will Feather."

After lunch, we displayed our pictures. We read aloud the things we had written about Jack. Then Miss Colman read *Make Way for Ducklings* to us. (I cried every time she said the name Jack.) When my teacher had finished the story, we stood by the windows. We looked into the courtyard. "I think we should say goodbye now," said Miss Colman.

"Goodbye. Goodbye, Jack," we whispered. The bell rang. School was over. I cried all the way home.

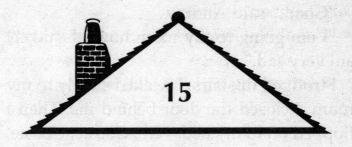

15

Karen's Sad Day

When I reached the little house, I ran through the front door. I was planning to run straight to my room. But Andrew stopped me.

"The post has already come," he said quietly.

"Uh-oh. Where is it?" I asked.

"On the table in the living room."

"Okay." I took a look at the post. I could not see any letters from the Custom Car Company. "Good," I said to Andrew. "Mr Simpson must have meant it when he said that was the last letter they would send."

"Good," said Andrew.

"I am going to my room now," I said. "I am very sad."

I trudged upstairs. I walked slowly to my room. I closed the door behind me. Then I flopped on to my bed. "Oh, Goosie, Goosie, Goosie." I cradled Goosie in my arms. I kissed his ears and his nose. "I do not like feeling sad," I told him. "I felt sad when Louie died. I felt sad when Crystal Light died. Now Jack has died. I wish animals and people did not have to die. But I guess they do. If nothing ever died, the Earth would be gigundoly crowded. Isn't that right, Goosie?" (I made Goosie nod his head.)

I sighed. Then I lay across my bed. I propped my feet up on the wall. I let my head hang over the edge. *"Somewhere over the rainbow,"* I sang, *"birds do fly. Birds fly over the rainbow. Why then, oh why, can't I?"* I felt just like Dorothy in *The Wizard of Oz,* when she was extra sad.

I sang as much of the song as I knew. When I could not remember any more words, I sat up. I moved to my desk. I found a pencil and a pad of paper. Then I thought for a while.

Finally I wrote *A Haiku for Jack*.

This was my haiku:

ONE FUZZY DUCKLING
WAS TOO LITTLE AND GOT SICK.
GOODBYE.   WE MISS YOU.

I liked my poem. But I decided to keep it private. At least for a while. I put it away. I put it in my best hiding place. And when I did that, I saw the letters and the broken car from the Custom Car Company.

"Oh," I groaned. I still felt bad about that car. Even if it had broken, Andrew and I should have paid for it. Not paying for it was like stealing.

I was a seven-year-old criminal.

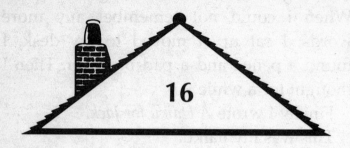

16

Spring Day

One morning, I woke up in my little-house bed. Before I did anything else, I looked out of my window. I saw sunshine. I saw a clear blue sky. I opened my window and felt warm air on my face.

"Yes!" I cried.

It was a perfect spring day. And it was perfect for celebrating Spring Day.

When Miss Colman had first started talking about Spring Day, I had thought it seemed so, so far away. Now it had arrived!

Nancy and I walked into our classroom

that morning feeling very important. Miss Colman had put our special spring projects on display. They were set up on tables and desks and the windowsills.

There were our zinnias in the milk cartons. They had sprouted and grown. And most of them had bloomed. (My zinnia flowers were red. Nancy's were pink. So were Hannie's.)

And there was our terrarium. It was sitting on Miss Colman's desk and it looked very beautiful. The plants were bright green. The violets had bloomed. They were guess what colour. (Violet.) And the moss looked damp and springy. Also, the terrarium was taking care of itself just like it was supposed to. The glass sides and the top of the aquarium were covered with droplets of water that would rain down on the plants and then collect on the glass again to make more rain.

And our bulletin board was finished. Our paper flowers looked very cheerful. Miss Colman had even let me make clouds out of cotton wool. Plus, we felt quite proud our poems, since we had worked hard on them.

Best of all, *Feather's Story* was on display, too. It was not finished, of course. (It would not be finished until Feather and her ducklings had left the courtyard.) But it was almost finished. We had made a cover for our big book. And we had put our drawings and photos inside the book to illustrate the first parts of the story.

In the morning, my classmates and I made a sign. It said, SPRING DAY IS HERE! We hung it on the blackboard. In the afternoon, Mr Berger and his class came to our room.

"Happy Spring Day!" we shouted.

Then each of us found a partner from Mr Berger's class. We showed our partners our spring projects. We told them what we had learned.

"These are my zinnias," I said to Liddie Yuan. "First they were just seeds. I planted the seeds in dirt, and I watered them a little

The seeds sprouted, and then ... grew, and then the flowers

...over here is our terrarium. . ."

A... a while, Mr Berger's class sat on the floor in the back of our room. My friends and I read some of our poems and stories aloud. We showed off our bulletin board. Then Miss Colman brought out *Feather's Story.*

"Ooh, look at that," said Liddie.

"A story about the duck," said someone else.

Miss Colman opened our book. On the very first page was a photo of Feather in the bushes, sitting on her nest of eggs. Miss Colman turned the page. She began to read the words we had written. First were Natalie's words. "Today is Tuesday. Yesterday Karen Brewer found a mummy duck in the garden." Miss Colman kept reading until she had read our last entry in Feather's diary, which was the entry from the day before.

"Feather's Story is not yet finished," Miss Colman told Mr Berger's students. "When it is finished, we will put it in the library. Then you can read the end of the book." She smiled. "Now Karen Brewer has something to say."

I stood up. "Thank you for coming to Spring Day," I said. "We hope you liked it." I paused. Then I added, "You have been wonderful guests."

Spring Day was over.

Trouble

Mummy was looking through the post. She was frowning.

"Is anything wrong?" I asked her.

She held up a letter. "This is something else about the Custom Car Company. It's so strange. I do not understand . . ." Mummy stopped talking. She read the letter. Then she read it again. She shook her head.

I edged around the kitchen table to my brother. I held Andrew's hand.

"I *tried* to get the post," he whispered me.

"*Shh*. It's okay," I replied.

I had come home from Spring Day feeling happy. I had almost forgotten about the fool car and policemen and jail. But here was a letter about the car. I was confused. I thought Mr Simpson said his last letter was going to *be* his last letter. Maybe I should have finished reading it.

"What does the letter say, Mummy?" I asked.

"Well, it is from a company whose business is to collect money from people who are not paying their bills. The Custom Car Company says I still owe them twenty-three ninety-five. Since I have not paid the money, they asked the bill company to get it from me."

Andrew's eyes filled with tears. "Are they going to rob our house?" he asked.

"Oh, no!" replied Mummy. "They just want me to send a cheque – badly."

y?" I asked. "Could you get ... you do not pay the bill?"

... know," said Mummy. "After all, ... ve the car. I did not order anything fro... e Custom Car Company. But Mr Simpson thinks I did. I will talk about this with Seth when he comes home."

Andrew and I went to my room. We closed the door.

"We got Mummy in trouble," I said.

Andrew nodded. "I know."

"I think there is only one thing we can do. We will have to tell Mummy the truth. Seth, too. We cannot let Mummy go to jail."

"Will *we* have to to go jail?" asked my brother. "We did something wrong."

I thought for a moment. Then I said, "We will have to take that risk."

Andrew and I waited until Seth came home from work. Then we went downstairs. "Mummy?" I said. "Seth? Andrew and I have to talk to you. About the Custom Car Company." Mummy raised her eyebrows.

"We know why you are getting those letters," I went on.

"And we do not want you to go to jail," added Andrew. "We love you."

I told Mummy and Seth the story about the cool red car. I told them everything. Then I took the broken car from its hiding place. "This is it," I said. "The car broke right away. Plus it cost twenty dollars, not two. Andrew and I did not know what to do."

"I wish you had told me this sooner," said Mummy.

"Me, too," I said.

"However," Mummy continued, "we can take care of the problem – without going to jail. I will pay for the car. But you two – " she pointed to Andrew and me – "will have to do extra chores to pay me back. And in the future, if you want something, talk to Seth or me about it. We might have been able to tell you the car was not well made. That is why it broke. And no more ordering things in other people's names. That is not

83

right. Now let's forget about the car and enjoy dinner."

"Okay," I said.

Andrew and I smiled. Nobody was going to jail!

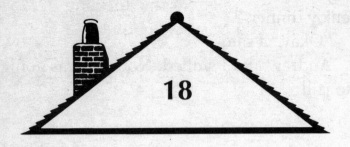

18

A Home for Feather

Feather's babies looked less like ducklings and more like ducks. I could tell that soon they would be ready to leave the courtyard.

"Miss Colman?" I said one day. "Who will take care of Feather after she and her babies leave our school? Oh, and could I have one of the ducklings? I promise to take really, really good care of it. I will keep it at Mummy's house. I love animals. I have two cats, two dogs and two fish. And I have my very own rat, Emily Junior. I always remember to feed her and give her fresh water and play with her. I bet Seth would help me make a pen for the duckling – "

"Karen," said Miss Colman.

"And when I am at the big house, Mummy would feed the duck."

"Karen – "

"Could I have Pack? I like that name."

"Karen," said my teacher for the third time.

"Yes?"

"No one is going to take Feather *or* her babies."

"Really?" I was surprised. "You mean they are going to stay at school?"

"No. We are going to let them go. Feather is wild. We have let her raise her babies as naturally as possible. So they are wild, too. They belong near a lake or a pond, where they can live on their own and meet other ducks and raise more ducklings. That is how they will be happiest."

"Oh."

I must have looked surprised and sad because Miss Colman said, "I thought you understood that, Karen. I thought you knew that is what would happen."

"I – I guess not," I stammered.

"Oh, dear. I wonder if any other students thought we were going to find homes for the ducks. I had better make an announcement."

Miss Colman talked to us about the ducks that morning. She explained that Feather and her babies were going to be set free. Then she said, "I have been talking to the people at SAPA about this. They will move the ducks to their new home. They will work very carefully, so the ducks will not be too scared."

Audrey raised her hand. "Where will their new home be?" she asked.

"It could be in several places. But the best place is Carnegie Lake. Do you know what that is? It is the small lake in Carnegie Park. The park is just outside Stoneybrook. I am sure most of you have been there for picnics."

"I know where it is!" I cried. (I forgot to

raise my hand.) "I have visited there lots of times. I like Carnegie Park."

"Do you think it is a good place for Feather and her ducklings?" asked Miss Colman.

"Yes," I replied.

"Does everyone agree that Carnegie Park should be the ducks' new home?"

"Yes!" we shouted.

"Wonderful. I think Feather will be very happy," said my teacher. "Soon we will let the ducks loose. I will call SAPA to find out the best day for that. Guess what. Our class will go to the park to watch the ducks when they see their new home. Maybe we should plan a 'Goodbye, Feather' morning."

So we did. We felt sad that the ducks were going to leave us. But we knew they would like Carnegie Park.

"They can swim in the lake as much as they want," said Ricky.

"And they can run wherever they want," said Natalie.

"*Feather's Story* will be over," I added.

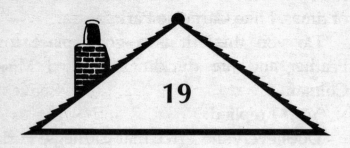

Good Luck, Feather!

I sniffed the air. It smelled like spring. And like woods. That made sense, since it was springtime and my friends and I were in the woods. We were in Carnegie Park. So was Miss Colman. So were three people from SAPA. And so were Feather and her babies.

The ducks were in two pens. The pens had come from SAPA. They were special pens for travelling animals.

Miss Colman and my classmates and I rode to the park in a school bus. The ducks rode in the SAPA animal van. The van followed our bus all the way to the park. We could not see Feather and her babies, but we knew they were behind us.

"This is the first trip the ducklings have ever taken," I said to Hannie and Nancy as we rode along. "It is probably Feather's first trip, too."

"Except for flying," Hannie answered. "We do not know where Feather has flown. Maybe she has flown around the world."

"Feather is smart," added Nancy, smiling. "We know *that* because she has been to school." Nancy giggled.

"I hope Feather is not too used to our school," I said. "What if she likes it better than Carnegie Lake?"

"She will like the lake," Hannie replied. "She will have duck friends there. I bet she was a little lonely at school."

Now we were walking through the woods to Carnegie Lake. I could smell damp soil and ferns and pine needles and dogwood blossoms. And soon I could

hear the noises of the lake – water lapping, frogs croaking, even a duck quacking.

"You are right," I said to Hannie. "Feather will have friends here."

When we reached the edge of the lake, we stopped. My classmates and I stood in a group. I was carrying a notebook and a pencil. I was going to write the very last part of *Feather's Story*. I hoped I could do it without crying. If I cried, my tears would blur my eyes and I would not be able to see what I was writing. I wanted to do a good job.

"Boys and girls, are you ready to say goodbye to Feather?" asked Miss Colman.

"Yes," we answered.

The people from SAPA carried the pens to the edge of the lake. The rest of us stood apart from them. Even then, we were not supposed to go near Feather or her babies. Only the animal people were allowed to do that.

"Nancy?" said Miss Colman.

Nancy stepped forward. She said, "Goodbye, Feather. We are glad you came to our school. You were a good friend. We are proud you decided to have your babies in the courtyard. We will miss all of you. Good luck!" (Nancy read her speech from a piece of paper.)

A man opened one of the pens. Out waddled Feather and two ducklings. He opened the other pen. Out waddled four ducklings. Feather stopped and stood still. The ducklings stopped and stood still too. Feather looked back at the pens. Then she looked at the water. After a moment, she waddled to the lake. The ducklings followed her. *Plop, plop, plop, plop, plop, plop, plop.* They hopped into the water. They swam away from us.

"Goodbye! Goodbye, Feather!" we called. And I added, "Goodbye, Kack, Lack, Mack, Nack, Oack, and Pack! And good luck!"

The ducks paddled off happily. Soon they were hidden by some tall weeds.

I wrote: "And they lived happily ever after. THE END."

I felt happy and sad. (I did not cry.)

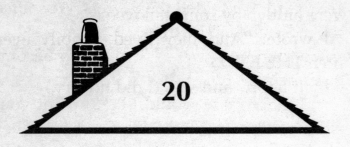

A Book for the Library

"Mmm. I smell flowers," said Hank.

"I smell grass," said Tammy.

"I smell springtime!" I exclaimed.

My classmates and I were back at school. Guess what. Miss Colman had opened the windows. And she had opened the door into the courtyard. We could do those things now that Feather and her babies were living at Carnegie Lake. I wished the ducks were still at school. But they were not, and I liked letting spring into our room.

Miss Colman even took us into the courtyard. We sniffed the flowers. We sniffed the blossoms on the trees.

We found out we were going to become gardeners.

"I thought you would like to plant your zinnias out here," said Miss Colman. "They cannot live in the milk cartons for ever. We could put the zinnias near Feather's nest. We could call that spot 'Feather's Garden'."

My friends and I liked the idea. We liked it very much. In fact, we planted Feather's Garden right away. When we had finished planting, it was time to finish something else. Our book.

First, I copied my end of the story into the end of the book. Here is how I wrote the last two words:

Then we put the rest of our pictures into the book. They were photos Miss Colman had taken at the lake that morning. They showed the ducks swimming away.

"Time to line up for the library," announced our teacher.

We ran to the door and formed a line. Miss Colman stood at the head of the line with our book. We marched proudly to the library.

"Hi, Mr Counts!" I called.

"Welcome," replied Mr Counts.

"We have a present for you," I announced. "I mean, for the library."

We crowded around Mr Counts' desk. Miss Colman placed the book on it.

"It is all finished," Ricky told Mr Counts.

"This is quite a book," replied our librarian. "May I read it?"

A bunch of nursery children were in the library. Mr Counts read *Feather's Story* to them. They laughed at some parts. They said, "That is so sad," at other parts. They asked questions about ducks.

"Your book is a success," Mr Counts told my class. Then he found a brand-new checkout card. He pasted a pocket inside the cover of our book. He slipped the card into the pocket.

"Next we will put information about *Feather's Story* in the card catalogue," he said. "That way, students can look up your book when they want to read about ducks."

My classmates and I were real, live, true authors. We had made a book. We had written it and illustrated it and bound it and made a cover for it. And now our book was in a library. Already, other kids had looked at it.

I turned to Hannie and Nancy, and I smiled. I smiled at Miss Colman. I smiled at Mr Counts. I smiled at the nursery children. But the nursery children did not see me. They were busy turning the pages of *Feather's Story*. They were arguing over who could borrow it first!

"I wonder what Feather and the ducklings

are doing right now," I said to Hannie. "I hope they are happy."

"I'm sure they are," Hannie replied. "They are where they belong."

I nodded. Then I said, "Feather made us happy. I am glad we could make her happy. And her babies."

Feather, I thought, I will never forget you.

Don't miss BLS 27

KAREN'S BIG JOKE

We looked in the box. I pulled out the plastic cockroach. "Do you know what I am going to do with this?" I asked Andrew. "I am going to take it to school on April Fool's Day Eve. I am going to get Bobby Gianelli with it. I will wait until gym is over. I will hide the bug in his shoe. Then when he takes off his sneakers and changes into his shoes, his foot will squish right on the bug!"

"Ew," said Andrew. He looked in the box again. He took out the trick soap and the trick gum and the trick ice cube and the rubber spider.

April Fool's Day was going to be gigundoly fun.

BABYSITTERS LITTLE SISTER

Meet Karen Brewer. She's seven years old and her big sister Kristy runs the Babysitters Club. And Karen's always having adventures of her own . . . Read all about her in her very own series.